A Collection
of
Love Poems

Christopher Poindexter

ISBN: 9798876128713

Printed in the United States of America

Cover design and book layout by Brittney Arthur

Jack Wild Publishing
www.jackwildpublishing.com

Above all,
I hope you know
how significant
you are.
I hope each kiss
tells you this.
I love you.
And I couldn't stop
if I tried.

You are more
than the love
of my life.
You are the love
of the life
before this one.
And you will be
the love of
the one after.

There is nothing
more powerful
on this earth
than finding
without a
shadow of
a doubt
the person
that feels
like an
extension
of your
own soul.

It takes
a special kind
of person
to make you
fall in love
with the
entire world.

Someone
to grow old
with.

Someone
to grow old
with.

Someone
to grow old
with.

It has become
more rare
these days.

But how beautiful
is the thought?

Loving someone
through decades
and decades
of both pain
and flowers.

In the spring I have
whispered your name in love
to the flowers

a heavenly wither
winter will not kill

by next spring they
will whisper back
your name in song

I am convinced
of one thing,
and only one thing
only—
love will be
the music of
my life.
To love
the earth,
the human,
the bird,
the worm.
Let supreme
tenderness
be the
beautiful melody.

No matter
the sorrow
and darkness
of what it means
to be fully human,
know this,
and know it well–
I will love,
I will love,
I will love.
It is my only
scripture
and religion.

And I can tell you
a thing
as sure as sun
and rain

I love you

with the same energy
the poets
notice the birds.

I just want you
to know above all
that I see you.
That I am proud
of your blossom
and healing.
That you have
always inspired me
to rise above myself
and become better,
my own river
of hope.
That you are not
merely a lover–
a teacher,
a muse,
a mentor,
a friend.

thy love,
I must tell you
I would give it all away,
send my earthly possessions,
my deepest longings and wants
somewhere where I may never
find them again,
if that is what was needed
to be yours.
I hang on that word like a prayer.
I whisper it to myself before
I fall asleep.
I am yours. I am yours. I am yours.
Yours. And no one else's.

simply
the sound
of her name
sends me to my knees.

I love you
simply because
I have no choice.
My body and mouth
do strange,
intoxicating things
when you are around
and there is no way
to stop it.
Trust me,
I've tried.

daydreaming
fondly of
deathbed love.
love that stays,
at all costs.

I've spent
my entire life
watching people being
happy,
hoping they truly are,
doing all I can
to illuminate the beauty
inside the other person.

In this
I have starved myself.
I have created
a mountainous void.

It is my time.
My chance at a revolution.

I want to ache
with acceptance,
romance,
and self love.

If you listen,
truly listen,
not a single day
goes by where
the earth
forgets to tell you
you are enough.

If they
tell you
you love and care
too much
it is them
who have something
wrong

the words
I love you
will never be
enough.
your essence
deserves more.
this is why a man
writes poetry.

The only thing
worth fighting for
is love.
This is the only
thing I am sure of.

In a few words,
if I were asked
how I love you,
why I love you,
and how I plan
to continue to love you
in a world where love
is tossed like leaves
in a rebellious fall,
I would reply
without a sliver
of hesitation,
in the same way hips
reply when making love,

"because loving you
is only my soul
telling my hands
what to do."

And even when you
are broken,
I will marry
your pieces.

I am
so in love
with you
it nearly
haunts me.

I love at her
and I know love.

I look away
and I know nothing.

There is
an ecstasy
that will
triumph
over all
ecstasies,
a river of
pure joy
that flows
when all
others
run dry–
to simply be
understood
by another
human.
To know without
words what
the other
desires truly.
What they cannot
live without.

I don't
care how dark
it all gets,
love is
and will always be
my answer.

There is one thing
I am sure of in this life,
and it has nothing to do
with the sorrow
I hold,
or the future pain
I will carry.
It is simply
and wholly this-
I will love
everthing
that must
be loved.
I will tend
to goodness.
No matter
the inevitable
weight of
my heart.

The space
between
not enough
and too much–

meet me there.

If you wish me
to be true I will
be true.

It is not that
I can't live
without you.

That has never been
the burden, the great
sorrow of my world.

I could go on,
get lost in other color,
love other bodies like
I love the rain.

If you wish me
to be true I will
be true.

It is not that
I can't live
without you.

It is simply that
I do not want to.

ABOUT THE AUTHOR

Christopher Poindexter is a poetic soul hailing from Southern Arkansas, whose verses resonate with the rhythm of jazz, channel the rebellious spirit of the Beat Generation, and draw inspiration from the enigmatic Arthur Rimbaud. Having explored diverse landscapes across the United States, Christopher now finds solace in Marietta, Ohio, where the town's historic charm and scenic beauty inspire his poetic pursuits. Christopher's commitment to exploring human emotions and connections remains unwavering. Through his poetry, he invites readers to introspect, find beauty in the mundane, and discover solace in the power of language. With each chapter of his life, Christopher Poindexter's poetic voice evolves, captivating readers in a celebration of the human experience.

Made in the USA
Las Vegas, NV
31 October 2024

10811232R00018